A Day of Rhymes

For Mum and Dad

A Red Fox Book
Published by Arrow Books Limited
20 Vauxhall Bridge Road, London SW1V 2SA

An imprint of the Random Century Group
London Melbourne Sydney Auckland
Johannesburg and agencies throughout the world

First published by The Bodley Head Ltd 1987
Red Fox edition 1990
Text and illustrations © Sarah Pooley 1987

Made and printed in Great Britain by
William Clowes Ltd, Beccles and London

ISBN 0 09 975110 0

A Day of Rhymes

Selected and Illustrated by
SARAH POOLEY

RING!   RING!

RED FOX

Here we go round the mulberry bush,
The mulberry bush, the mulberry bush,
Here we go round the mulberry bush,
On a cold and frosty morning.

This is the way we wash ourselves, etc.

This is the way we brush our teeth, etc.

Brush, Brush, Brush!

This is the way we put on our clothes, etc.

Elsie Marley is grown so fine,
She won't get up to feed the swine,
But lies in bed till eight or nine.
Lazy Elsie Marley.

Frère Jacques. Frère Jacques.
Dormez-vous? Dormez-vous?
Sonnez les matines! Sonnez les matines!
Ding Dang Dong.
Ding Dang Dong.

Pease porridge hot,
Pease porridge cold,
Pease porridge in the pot
Nine days old.
Some like it hot,
Some like it cold,
Some like it in the pot
Nine days old.

Through the teeth
Past the gums
Look out, stomach
Here it comes!

Thirty days hath September,
April, June, and November;

All the rest have thirty-one,
Excepting February alone,

And that has twenty-eight days clear
And twenty-nine in each leap year.

Spring is showery, flowery, bowery
Summer is hoppy, croppy, poppy
Autumn is wheezy, sneezy, freezy
Winter is slippy, drippy, nippy.

Round and round the garden
Like a teddy bear;
One step, two step,
Tickle you under there!

Mary, Mary, quite contrary,
How does your garden grow?
With silver bells and cockle shells,
And pretty maids all in a row.

Ring a ring o' roses,
A pocket full of posies,
A-tishoo, a-tishoo,
We all fall down.

Flowers grow like this,
Trees grow like this;
I grow
Just like that!

ZZZZZZ...

What do you suppose?
A bee sat on my nose.
Then what do you think?
He gave me a wink
And said, 'I beg your pardon,
I thought you were the garden.'

Two little dicky birds,
Sitting on a wall;
One named Peter,
The other named Paul.
Fly away, Peter!
Fly away, Paul!
Come back, Peter!
Come back, Paul!

BOO HOO!

Nobody loves me
Everybody hates me
I'll think I'll go and eat worms

Big fat squishy ones
Little thin skinny ones
See how they wriggle and squirm

Bite their heads off
'Schlurp!' they're lovely
Throw their tails away

SPIT!

Nobody knows
How big I grows
on worms three times a day.

Mmm....
worm pie...
worm soup...

Ladybird, ladybird,
Fly away home,
Your house is on fire
And your children are gone;
All except one
And that's little Ann
And she has crept under
The warming pan.

There was a little grasshopper
That was always on the jump,
And because he never looked ahead
He always got a bump.

Little Arabella Miller
Had a fuzzy caterpillar.
First it climbed upon her mother,
Then upon her baby brother.
They said,

YUK!

ARABELLA MILLER,
PUT AWAY YOUR
CATERPILLAR!

TE HE TE HE!

Pretty little butterfly, yellow as bright gold,
My sweet little butterfly, you sure are mighty bold.
You can dance out in the sun, you can fly up high,
But you know I'm bound to get you, yet, my little butterfly.

Rain, rain, go away,
Come again another day,
Little Johnny wants to play.
Rain, rain, go to Spain,
Never show your face again.

Incy Wincy Spider climbed up the water spout,
Down came the rain drops and washed poor Incy out;
Out came the sunshine and dried up all the rain,
And Incy Wincy Spider climbed up that spout again.

Chop, chop, choppity-chop,
Cut off the bottom,
And cut off the top.
What there is left we will
Put in the pot;
Chop, chop, choppity-chop.

Hickory, dickory, dock,
The mouse ran up the clock.
The clock struck one,
The mouse ran down,
Hickory, dickory, dock.
Tick tock, tick tock.

I eat my peas with honey.
I've done it all my life.
It makes the peas taste funny,
But it sticks them on the knife.

BEST
HONEY
(for keeping
peas on
your
knife)

Wish I was a little grub
with whiskers round my tummy.
I'd climb into a honey-pot
and make my tummy gummy.

Five little peas in a pea-pod pressed,
One grew, two grew and so did all the rest.
They grew and grew and they did not stop,
Until all of a sudden the pod went POP!

CLAP!

Ten fat sausages sizzling in the pan;
One went POP! and another went BANG!

Eight fat sausages, etc.

One potato, two potato,
Three potato, four,
Five potato, six potato,
Seven potato, more!

Mr East gave a feast
Mr North laid the cloth;
Mr West did his best
Mr South burnt his mouth
With eating a cold potato.

Jelly on the plate,
Jelly on the plate.
Wibble, wobble,
Wibble, wobble,
Jelly on the plate.

S-C-R-E-A-M!

I scream, you scream,
We all scream
For ICE-CREAM!

The wheels on the bus go round and round,
Round and round, round and round.
The wheels on the bus go round and round,
All day long.

The horn on the bus goes peep, peep, peep, etc.

The windscreen wiper on the bus goes swish, swish, swish, etc.

The people on the bus bounce up and down, etc.

An elephant goes like this and that.
He's terribly big,
And he's terribly fat.
He has no fingers,
And he has no toes,
But goodness gracious, what a nose!

Down in the grass, coiled up in a heap,
Lies a fat snake, fast asleep.
When he hears the grasses blow,
He moves his body to and fro.
Up and down and in and out,
Watch him slowly move about!
Now his jaws are open, so—
Ouch! He's caught my finger! Oh!

HOW-DO   YOU-DO!

TWEET!
TWEET!

TWEET!

Two fat gentlemen met in a lane,
Bowed most politely, bowed once again.
How do you do,
How do you do,
And how do you do again?

Two thin ladies met in a lane, etc.

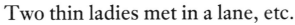

HOW-DO   YOU-DO!

HOW-DO YOU-DO!

Two tall postmen met in a lane, etc.

Two little schoolboys met in a lane, etc.

HOW-DO YOU-DO!

Two little babies met in a lane, etc.

HOW-DO   YOU-DO!

One, two, three, four, five,
Once I caught a fish alive,
Six, seven, eight, nine, ten,
Then I let it go again.
Why did you let it go?
Because it bit my finger so.
Which finger did it bite?
This little finger on the right.

Row, row, row your boat,
Gently down the stream.
Merrily, merrily, merrily, merrily;
Life is but a dream.

Ali-Baba has a farm.
On that farm he has some cows.
'Moo, Moo,' say the cows
On Ali-Baba's farm.

MOO!

MOO!

Ali-Baba has a farm.
On that farm he has some sheep.
'Baa, Baa,' say the sheep
On Ali-Baba's farm.

BAA!
BAA!

COCK-A-DOODLE-DO!

Ali-Baba has a farm.
On that farm he has some cocks.
'Cock-a-doodle-doo,' say the cocks
On Ali-Baba's farm.

GEE-UP!

NEIGH!

Ali-Baba has a farm
On that farm he has some horses.
'Neigh, Neigh,' say the horses
On Ali-Baba's farm.

OINK! OINK!

This little piggy went to market,

This little piggy stayed at home,

This little piggy had roast beef,

This little piggy had none,

And this little piggy cried, Wee-wee-wee-wee-wee,

All the way home.

Have you seen the little ducks
Swimming in the water?
Mother, father, baby ducks,
Grand-mamma and daughter.

Have you seen them dip their bills,
Swimming in the water?, etc.

Have you seen them flap their wings,
Swimming in the water?, etc.

DACY STORES

Tall shop in the town,
Lifts moving up and down.
Doors swinging round about,
People going in and out.

Here is the church,
Here is the steeple,
Open the doors
And here are the people.

Knock at the door,
Pull the bell,
Lift the latch,
And walk in.

These are Grandmother's glasses,
This is Grandmother's hat;
Grandmother folds her hands like this,
And lays them in her lap.

These are Grandfather's glasses,
This is Grandfather's hat;
This is the way he folds his arms,
And has a little nap.

Pat-a-cake, pat-a-cake,
Baker's man,
Bake me a cake
As fast as you can.
Pat it and prick it
And mark it with B,
And put it in the oven
For Baby and me.

Mix a pancake,
Stir a pancake,
Pop it in the pan.

Fry the pancake,
Toss the pancake,
Catch it if you can!

Grandma's baked a cake for me.
See the candles, one, two, three.
Put them out with one big blow.
Ready, steady, here we go.

My shoes are new and squeaky shoes,
They're very shiny, creaky shoes,
I wish I had my leaky shoes
That mummy threw away.

I liked my old brown leaky shoes
Much better than these creaky shoes,
These shiny, creaky, squeaky shoes
I've got to wear today.

GLUG!

I'm a little teapot, short and stout;
Here's my handle, here's my spout.
When I see the tea-cups, hear me shout,
'Tip me up and pour me out.'

This is the way the ladies ride,
Trit, trot, trit, trot.
This is the way the gentlemen ride,
Jiggety-jog, jiggety-jog.
This is the way the farmers ride,
Hobblety-hoy, hobblety-hoy.
This is the way the hunters ride,
Gallopy, gallopy, tripperty trot,
Till they fall in a ditch with a flipperty flop!

Gee up!

Gee up!

Rub-a-dub-dub,
Three men in a tub,
And who do you think they be?
The butcher, the baker,
The candlestick-maker,
Turn them out, knaves all three!

Head, shoulders, knees and toes
Knees and toes
Head, shoulders, knees and toes
Knees and toes
And eyes and ears and mouth and nose
Head and shoulders, knees and toes
Knees and toes.

Three little monkeys jumping on the bed
One fell off and banged her head
Mummy called the doctor and the doctor said:
'No more monkeys jumping on the bed!'

Two little monkeys, etc.

THERE! THERE!

Miss Polly had a dolly
Who was sick, sick, sick.
So she phoned for the doctor
To come quick, quick, quick.

COME QUICK!

The doctor came
With her bag and her hat,
And she rapped on the door
With a rat-tat-tat.

She looked at the dolly
And she shook her head
Then she said, 'Miss Polly,
Put her straight to bed.'

RAT-A-

TAT-TAT!

She wrote on a paper
For a pill, pill, pill.
'I'll be back in the morning
With my bill, bill, bill.'

OH DEAR!

BYE-EE!

Diddle, diddle, dumpling, my son John,
Went to bed with his trousers on;
One shoe off, and one shoe on,
Diddle, diddle, dumpling, my son John.

Wee Willie Winkie runs through the town,
Upstairs and downstairs in his night-gown,
Rapping at the window, crying through the lock,
Are the children all in bed, for now it's eight o'clock.

There were ten in the bed,
And the little one said,
Roll over, roll over.
So they all rolled over,
And one fell out.

Roll over!

There were nine in the bed, etc, until . . .

There was one in the bed,
And he said,
Roll over, roll over.
So he rolled over,
And he fell out.
There were none in the bed,
So nobody said,
Roll over, roll over.

Hush, little baby, don't say a word,
Papa's going to buy you a mocking bird.

And if that mocking bird don't sing,
Papa's going to buy you a diamond ring.

And if that diamond ring turns to brass,
Papa's going to buy you a looking-glass.

And if that looking-glass gets broke,
Papa's going to buy you a billy-goat.

And if that billy-goat don't pull,
Papa's going to buy you a cart and bull.

And if that cart and bull turn over,
Papa's going to buy you a dog named Rover.
And if that dog named Rover don't bark,
Papa's going to buy you a horse and cart.

And if that horse and cart fall down,
You'll still be the sweetest little baby in town.

Go to bed late,
Stay very small;
Go to bed early,
Grow very tall.

Five little owls in an old elm-tree,
Fluffy and puffy as owls could be,
Blinking and winking with big round eyes
At the big round moon that hung in the skies:
As I passed beneath, I could hear one say,
'There'll be mouse for supper, there will, to-day!'
Then all of them hooted 'To-whit, To-whoo!
Yes, mouse for supper, Hoo hoo, Hoo hoo!'

Hey diddle, diddle,
The cat and the fiddle,
The cow jumped over the moon;
The little dog laughed
To see such sport,
And the dish ran away with the spoon.

Twinkle, twinkle, little star,
How I wonder what you are!
Up above the world so high,
Like a diamond in the sky.

Index of First Lines